Walt Disney's Winnie the Pooh
HALF A HAYCORN PIE

By Betty Birney
Illustrated by Darrell Baker

A GOLDEN BOOK • NEW YORK

Western Publishing Company, Inc., Racine, Wisconsin 53404

Piglet loved haycorns more than any other food in the Hundred-Acre Wood. In fact, Piglet loved haycorns almost as much as his friend Winnie the Pooh loved honey.

Hardly a day went by that Piglet didn't make a haycorn pie or a haycorn stew or even a haycorn-and-jelly sandwich.

Piglet even loved the little cups the haycorns sat in. He had haycorn baskets and haycorn picture frames and haycorn whatnots and knickknacks all over his house.

So it wasn't unusual for Piglet to wake up with a
craving for haycorns, as he did one morning in particular.
And it wasn't unusual for Piglet to take his basket and go
searching for haycorns, either. But what was unusual was
that Piglet didn't find a single haycorn.

There were haycorn trees everywhere, but—much to
Piglet's disappointment—not a nut to be found.

"I'll bet a horrible Heffalump has stolen them all!"
Piglet thought when he got back home.

Then he sat and began to wonder if there were any haycorns left anywhere in the world. "What a terrible place the world would be with no haycorns in it," thought Piglet.

No haycorns for pies or stews or sandwiches! No haycorn trees to provide shade or homes for birds or places to climb.

"You don't look very happy, Piglet," said Winnie the Pooh when he and Rabbit and Eeyore came to call on their friend.

Piglet explained how there were no more haycorns left in the Hundred-Acre Wood and how very sad that made him.

"There are always haycorns," said Rabbit. "We'll help you find some!"

So Eeyore, Rabbit, Pooh, and Piglet went hiking through the forest.

Pooh found a lovely tree with a hive just dripping with sweet golden honey.

But he didn't find any haycorns.

Eeyore found a field filled with prickly purple thistles.
"Mighty tasty," he said as he munched away.
But he didn't find any haycorns.

Rabbit was determined to find some haycorns for Piglet. So when he didn't find any *on* the ground, he began to dig *under* the ground.

Eventually he found four haycorns.

"I told you I'd find some," he bragged.

"Not so loud," whispered Piglet. "There might be a horrible haycorn-stealing Heffalump nearby."

Rabbit offered the four haycorns to Piglet.

"Thank you, Rabbit," said Piglet. "There's one for each of us."

Rabbit, Pooh, and Eeyore quickly popped their haycorns into their mouths.

But Piglet just held his haycorn and looked at it.
"Aren't you going to eat it?" asked Pooh in amazement.
"Not yet," replied Piglet.

When he got home again, Piglet carefully planted his
haycorn in a special spot right outside his front door.

Pooh scratched his head. "Piglet, I thought you liked
haycorns to eat."

"I do," his friend replied as he tenderly covered his haycorn with dirt. "But I want to have haycorns to eat in the future. And if I plant this one nut, in time it will grow into a tree with hundreds and hundreds of delicious haycorns!"

Piglet spent most of the day watching the spot where his haycorn was planted. He was waiting for it to grow.

Suddenly Piglet heard a strange sound! He began to shake. "Oh, no!" he thought. "It's probably that horrible haycorn-stealing Heffalump!"

But it wasn't a Heffalump at all. It was Tigger and Roo. They came bouncing into his front yard, carrying basket after basket filled to the brim with crunchy golden haycorns!

"Surprise!" said Roo. "We got up early this morning and picked all these for you."

Piglet looked at the haycorns and sighed. "I'm glad you're not a horrible Heffalump," he said. "But no wonder I couldn't find any haycorns in the Hundred-Acre Wood today!"

"We were kind of hoping you'd bake us one of your
Tiggerific haycorn pies," said Tigger, smacking his lips.

"Mmmm, mmmm," agreed Roo, patting his tummy.

"I don't think I can do that," said Piglet.

"You can't?" said Tigger, disappointed. "But why?"

Piglet thought for a bit and then announced, "I know.
I'll bake *half* a haycorn pie."

Tigger and Roo both looked puzzled, so Piglet explained.

"From now on, I'm planning to plant one haycorn for every haycorn I eat. That way I'll never again have to worry about a world without haycorns."

Soon Piglet's friends were all merrily helping him plant haycorns in the Hundred-Acre Wood.

Piglet's half a haycorn pies have become famous in the Hundred-Acre Wood. And every time Piglet or Pooh or any of their friends take a bite of half a haycorn pie, they know there will be many more half a haycorn pies to look forward to in the future. Somehow that makes the one they are eating taste even better than before!